Amazing & Incredible Counting Stories!

A NUMBER OF TALL TALES

Max Grover

Browndeer Press
Harcourt Brace & Company
SAN DIEGO NEW YORK LONDON

For all who have found the Oasis

—Max

Library of Congress Cataloging-in-Publication Data
Grover, Max.
Amazing & incredible counting stories/Max Grover.—1st ed.
p. cm.
"Browndeer press."
Summary: Hypothetical newspaper headlines, on subjects ranging
from missing skyscrapers to a radio refrigerator, introduce counting.
ISBN 0-15-200090-9
[1. Newspapers—Fiction. 2. Counting.] I. Title.
II. Title: Amazing and incredible counting stories.
PZ7.G93113Am 1995
[E]—dc20 94-17837

PRINTED IN SINGAPORE

First edition
A B C D E

The paintings in this book were done in acrylics on D'Arches Lavis Fedelis drawing paper.
The display and text type were set in Franklin Gothic Condensed.
Color separations were made by Bright Arts, Ltd., Singapore.
Printed by Tien Wah Press, Singapore
This book was printed on Leykam recycled paper, which contains more than 20 percent
postconsumer waste and has a total recycled content of at least 50 percent.
Production supervision by Warren Wallerstein and David Hough
Designed by Michael Farmer

Skyscrapers Missing, 1 Found

Most of downtown's tall buildings disappeared during yesterday's power failure, but a search party found this beauty near the edge of town.

Sleepless Resident

These battling instruments angered neighbors with loud playing over Maple Street last night.

pset by 2 Giant Banjos

As a result of the noisy music, the thunderstorm that blew down several trees went unnoticed.

Fleet of 3 Blimps Ready to Clean Skies

These new vacuums were launched by the city today in an effort to clean up the air downtown. Engineers are still working on ways to keep the cords plugged in.

4 Jelly Faucets Prove Big Time-Saver for Kids

A girl shows how quickly she can make sandwiches using this new device. Now she has more time to spend with her pet alligator.

Game Show Contestant Wins 5 Toasters

This lucky man recently took home these valuable appliances. His breakfast-loving children helped him beat the competition.

6 Radio Refrigerators Keep Them Dancing

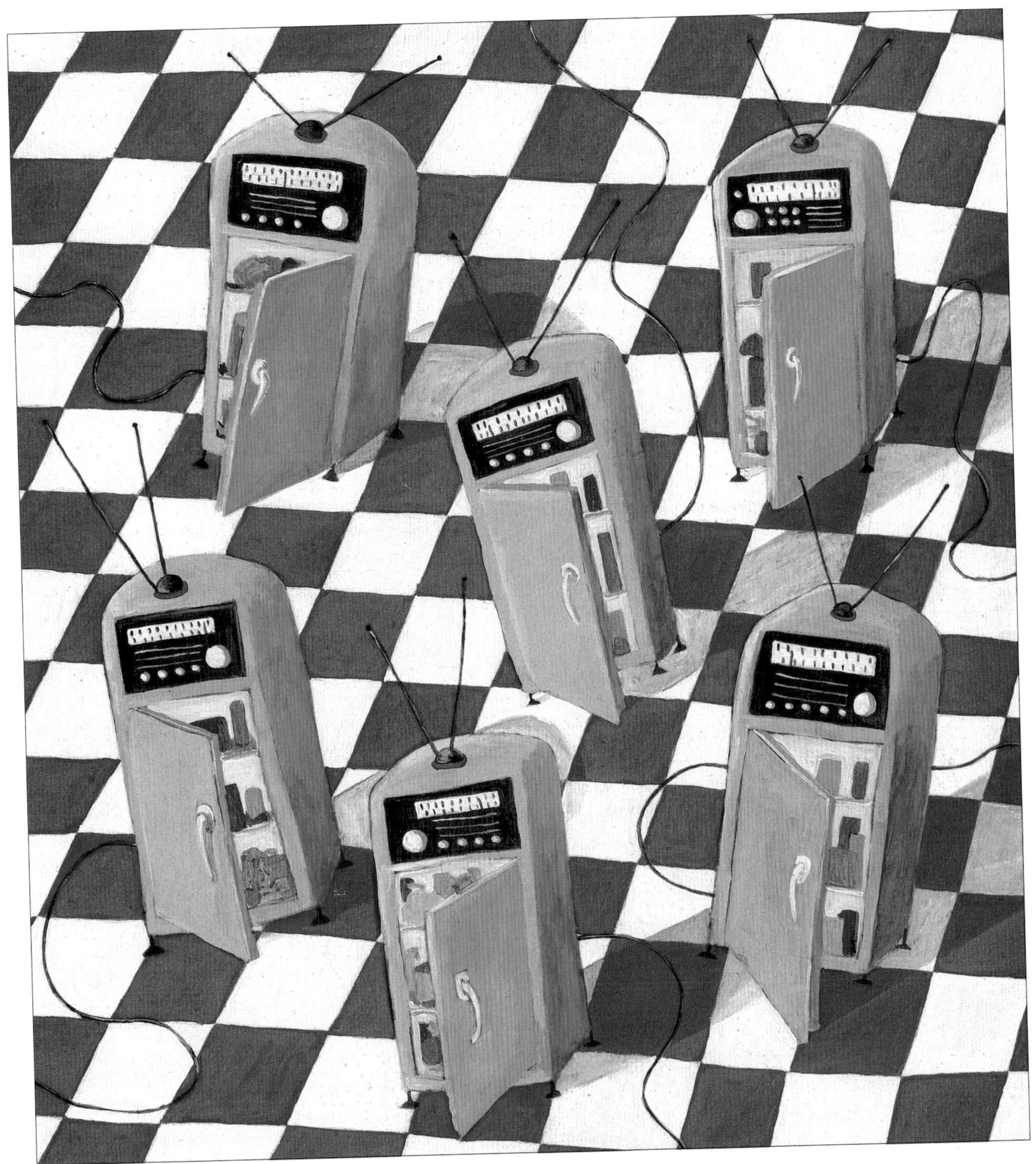

These unusual chilling devices keep food informed and entertained throughout the day. The food stays cool when the music gets hot.

7 Barges Set to Sail Today

These loaded barges patiently wait in the harbor to begin their long journey. The furniture is traveling this way because it's too far to walk.

8 Carrot Icicles Form on Roof Overnight

Yesterday this family bought a new dessert cookbook. Thanks to the timely appearance of these unusual vegetables, they will have iced carrot cake today.

Young Genius Develops 9-Piece Lollipop

Frustrated that his candy never lasted long enough, this inventor came up with a solution. "I hope my creation gets lots of looks and licks," he said.

Banana Boat with Crew of 10 Arrives

The sailors aboard the luxury craft *Yellow Bunch* are here to repair the brown spots that appear on their ship in warm weather.

11 Telephones Found Growing in Woods

Hikers discovered this unusual tree when they heard ringing in the forest, but by the time they arrived on the scene the caller had hung up.

12 Ready to Move into House with 13 Chimneys

This large family looks forward to a cozy winter in their new home. The extra chimney is for guests.

14-Piece Spoon Necklace Shocks Fashion World

This model shows off a stunning example of designer jewelry. Onlookers had to eat their soup with forks.

15 Doughnuts Appear to Be UFO's

What many people believed were flying saucers turned out to be tasty snacks. These people like to juggle before eating.

Auto with 16 Whee

Much fanfare and excitement greeted this new car as it left the showroom yesterday.

n One Side Set to Roll

Some people said the unusual color caused the commotion.

17-Layer Cake Baked for Party

A huge cake was featured at this pole-vaulter's birthday. His talent came in handy when it was time to blow out the candles.

Display to Feature 18-Rocket Spectacular

These fireworks stand ready for tonight's event in the park. The spectacle is held every year to celebrate the start of bowling season.

19-Member Accordion Troop Returns

These amazing acrobats are back for their annual show at the fairgrounds. They will perform many old favorites, including the Pyramid Polka, shown here.

Vendor Sells 20 Balloons in Minutes

This amusement park vendor sells out his new-and-improved inflatable pickles in a flash. Some observers noted they strongly resemble last year's favorite—inflatable cucumbers.

Bed with 21 Mattresses Arrives in Town

The president of the local mountain-climbing club is shown here with the country's tallest bunk bed. Whoever gets the top bunk will really be lucky!

22 Scientists Stumped by 23-Piece Puzzle

This unusual jigsaw puzzle made of linoleum has baffled some of our greatest minds. Some believe there are too many pieces; others think there are not enough scientists.

24-Hose Hydrant Installed

This new fire-fighting device went into service today. Octopuses looking for work should contact the mayor's office.

Miracle Airplane Shower Saves 25 Trees

The recent dry spell threatened this grove of orange trees. The new method of watering will not only save crops—it will help keep the pilots clean.

50 Shoes Run Wild Down Main Street

Numerous footprints turned up in this freshly paved sidewalk. This herd of footwear is believed to be responsible.

Perfect Time Kept by 75-Clock Castle

After being closed for repairs, the world-famous Tick-Tock Palace is again a popular destination for travelers, who come to see what time it is and set their watches.

Factory Produces 10

The Yellow Yardstick Company set a new world record for the 100-yardstick dash this week!

ardsticks at a Time

Workers said it was team spirit that helped them reach the milestone.

Millions of Readers Learn by Counting Stories!

Downtown streets were filled with readers eager to improve their counting skills. The main library had to close early because all of its books were checked out.